A Fairy
Merry Christmas

FAIRY SCHOOL

A Fairy
Merry
Christmas

by Gail Herman

illustrated by Laura Maestro

A Skylark Book

New York • Toronto • London • Sydney • Auckland

RL 2.5, AGES 006–009

A FAIRY MERRY CHRISTMAS

A Bantam Skylark Book / October 2000

ISBN 0-553-48737-X

Visit us on the Web! www.randomhouse.com/kids

Educators and librarians, for a variety of teaching tools, visit us at www.randomhouse.com/teachers

Published simultaneously in the United States and Canada

BANTAM SKYLARK is an imprint of Random House Children's Books, a division of Random House, Inc. SKYLARK BOOK and colophon and BANTAM BOOKS and colophon are registered trademarks of Random House, Inc. Bantam Books, 1540 Broadway, New York, New York 10036.

PRINTED IN THE UNITED STATES OF AMERICA

CWO   0 9 8 7 6 5 4 3 2 1

A Fairy
Merry Christmas

Chapter 1

"**H**ey! Watch it, fairy!"

Dorrie Windmist glanced back. Laurel, another little fairy, was sitting behind her and frowning.

"I'm sorry," Dorrie said. "I don't mean for my hair to fly in your face. It just keeps blowing in the wind." She tried to tuck her long unruly curls behind her ears. "There! That should do it!"

1

Dorrie grinned at her friends. Trina Larkspur, Belinda Dentalette, and Olivia Skye were sitting in a row beside her. The tiny fairies, along with the entire first-grade class from Fairy School, were riding on Blitzen, one of Santa's reindeer. They were on their way to the North Pole for a class trip.

"Look at those pretty ice-capped mountains," called their teacher, Ms. Periwinkle. "Earth-Below can be so beautiful! It's nice to travel from Fairyland for a visit."

Dorrie twisted to smile at Trina again and almost slipped off Blitzen's furry back.

"Oops!" she said.

"You should sit still," Trina told her seriously. "It's easy to fall off and get left behind. You know fairies can't fly nearly as fast as reindeer."

Dorrie laughed. "Especially if you're as clumsy as I am. But I can't sit still! I'm too excited!"

Dorrie's taller sister, Arianna, had told Dorrie about *her* class trip to the North Pole, so Dorrie knew just what to expect. A guided tour of the workshop, a peek into the reindeer stables, and a delicious lunch—all hosted by Santa Claus. Dorrie couldn't wait.

Dorrie's hair whipped in the wind, slapping Laurel in the face again.

"You're more than clumsy," Laurel grumbled. "You're ridiculous—like that bumblebee who lives next door to my tree-house, always getting stuck in his own honey."

"Say anything you want, Laurel," Dorrie said to the mean fairy. "Even you can't bother me today. Christmas is tomorrow. We're going to meet Santa right now. I'm so happy, I could—"

"Jump up and down until the next full moon?" suggested Belinda.

"I'm sure *you* could do that," Dorrie laughed. "But I don't have that much energy."

3

"Me neither," Olivia agreed softly. "But I'm excited too. Imagine, we'll get to see all the elves' handiwork—carving, painting—right up close. The toys they make are real works of art."

"Do you know Santa and his elves begin making toys on January second and don't stop until Christmas Eve?" Trina said, flipping through one of the books she'd taken from her fairypack.

"I wonder if we'll see them load the sleigh," Dorrie said. "Maybe we'll even get a ride! I'd love that!"

"Loading the sleigh. Let's see . . . ," Trina murmured, thumbing through the book. "There! On average, that takes three hours, twelve minutes."

Dorrie patted Trina's wing. She was glad they were partners for this trip. It seemed as if Trina had all the answers.

Blitzen made a sharp right turn, and Dorrie grabbed Trina's arm so she wouldn't tumble off.

"Get set for the landing!" Blitzen called to the fairies as he swooped down toward a warm, glowing light.

Santa's home!

Chapter 2

Dorrie tumbled off Blitzen's back and landed in a soft pile of snow. A red-haired elf wearing a long red scarf scooped her up and held her in his palm.

"Are you all right, little fairy?" he asked.

Dorrie giggled. "Sure I am. You must be Clyde, the chief elf." Arianna had told her that the head elf always wore red and that every toy he painted was bright red too.

6

"That's me," said Clyde. He gave a quick smile to the fairies, then turned to Ms. Periwinkle. "If you'll follow me, I'll take you around the workshop." He checked his pocket watch, which dangled from a chain. "We don't have much time, so let's get going."

Clyde was showing them the workshop? Not Santa? Dorrie was surprised. Santa had taken Arianna's class there—and he'd let them spend all morning playing with the toys.

"That's okay," Dorrie told herself. "Santa will probably show us the reindeer stables. And then we'll all eat lunch!"

"This way, this way," Clyde said, ushering the class through the workshop door. "And watch your wings, please. This place can get pretty crazy."

"That's for sure!" Dorrie whispered to Trina.

A big round table sat in the middle of the floor. Grouchy-looking elves were working furiously at every seat. Other elves scurried here and there, handing out paints and brushes, nails and screws, and scissors and ribbon. Hammers pounded. Wrapping paper fluttered.

Dorrie gazed wide-eyed at the human-sized toys that covered every inch of the floor.

Olivia stepped inside a dollhouse. "Would anyone like some tea?" she asked, holding up a teapot and cup.

Belinda dove into a toy boat. "Or would you rather go for a sail?"

"I'm going to ride the train!" Dorrie shouted, hopping aboard a shiny black engine. "Look! It has real controls." She leaned closer to examine the knobs and buttons.

Roar! The engine sprang to life.

"Oh, no!" she cried. "I started it by accident!" The train leaped forward. "How do you steer this thing?"

"You can't!" Clyde shouted. "It needs

tracks! They must be here somewhere." He desperately searched for a box of tracks among the gifts as the train chugged straight ahead. Faster, faster. It was picking up speed.

"Watch out!" Trina called to Dorrie. "You're headed right for—"

Crash! The train barreled into a pile of teddy bears. Then it stopped.

Trina, Olivia, and Belinda rushed over, fluttering their wings worriedly.

"Are you all right under there?" Trina called.

Dorrie poked her head out from among the bears and grinned. "Sure! These teddy bears are so soft! I wish they came fairy-sized!"

Clyde crossed his arms and frowned. "I think this tour is over, Ms. Periwinkle."

"Yes, yes, of course," Ms. Periwinkle murmured, drawing her fairy students in close. "We're sorry for any inconvenience."

"Yes," Dorrie said, hanging her head. "I'm sorry I messed things up."

"That's all right," Clyde said, softening. "It's just that this year, things are a bit ... different, and I'm under a little strain."

"Different?" Dorrie repeated to herself. What exactly did he mean?

Before she could ask, a sweet voice swept through the room.

"Ho, ho, ho! Are there any fairies here?"

"It's Mrs. Claus!" Trina exclaimed.

Mrs. Claus bounded into the room. She tucked her curly gray hair under a stocking cap and grinned at the fairies. "Hello, everyone. How is your visit so far?"

"It's wonderful," said Ms. Periwinkle.

Dorrie waved her arm at the jumble of teddy bears. "But I'm afraid I've made a mess."

"Well, accidents happen," Mrs. Claus said cheerfully. "And if I know your teacher, she'll put things in order quicker than you can say Merry Christmas."

Dorrie turned hopefully to Ms. Periwinkle. The teacher nodded, then waved her magic wand at the teddy bears. *"Teddy bears, teddy bears on the floor. Straighten up, just like before,"* she chanted.

Immediately the bears popped up from the floor and landed in a neat pile.

"Thank you," Dorrie said.

"Now that's taken care of," said Mrs. Claus, "let's leave the workshop. I'll take you to the stables to meet the other reindeer, and then we'll go to the house for a snack."

Mrs. Claus was giving the tour? And they'd just have a snack, not lunch?

What was going on?

A little while later, the first-grade fairies flew into the Clauses' cozy home. Cookies and milk were already set up on long wooden building blocks. Everything was just the right size.

"The reindeer were all so nice!" Dorrie told her friends as they settled down to eat. "And that Rudolph! He can sure tell jokes."

"Too bad the reindeer aren't allowed to talk to anybody on Earth-Below," Trina said. "Everyone would be laughing so hard, it would be the jolliest holiday ever!"

Dorrie looked around. "Now Santa will join us, I'm sure. Even if it's just for a snack. Arianna told me he never misses a meal!

She reached for a cookie. "Yum. Chocolate chip. My favorite!" she added, thanking Mrs. Claus.

It was nice to sit and rest after flying around the stables and seeing all the sights at the North Pole. In fact, Dorrie thought, they'd seen everything and met everyone— except for Santa Claus.

She munched on the cookie, expecting

him to show up any minute. But when the cookies and milk were gone and the fairies had helped clean up, there was still no sign of Santa.

"Where *is* he?" Dorrie whispered worriedly to Trina.

"You're wondering about Santa?" asked Mrs. Claus, bustling over. "He's busy waxing the sleigh for the ride."

"Oh," said Dorrie. Mrs. Claus had a funny expression, almost as if she didn't believe what she'd just said. Almost as if she had something to hide.

Dorrie flew her plate to the human-sized kitchen sink and put it down carefully. She didn't want to make any sort of mess—not again.

A giant soap bubble suddenly rose from the suds. Before Dorrie knew what was happening, she was caught inside the bubble.

"Trina!" she called. "Help!"

Trina flew after Dorrie as the bubble carried her down the hall.

"Just pop it!" Trina called, trying to keep up.

"Of course!" Dorrie reached for her magic wand and burst the bubble. She dropped through the air before she could flutter her wings and catch herself. "Uh-oh," she said, tumbling against a half-open door.

The door opened a bit more, and Dorrie stumbled inside. A Big Person was sitting at a desk by a blazing fire.

"Santa Claus!"

Chapter 3

Trina flitted into the room beside Dorrie. "What's going on?" she asked.

"We're in Santa Claus's special study!" Dorrie whispered. "And I think Santa wants to be alone. We should go."

"Who's there?" Santa called. "Clyde, is that you?"

"No," Dorrie said reluctantly. "It's just us. Two fairies visiting from Fairy School."

She and Trina flew farther into the room. Santa's cheeks looked pale instead of rosy. His curly beard drooped. He gazed sadly at the fairies, then nodded slowly.

"Hello, Dorrie. Hello, Trina," he said quietly.

"You know our names?" Dorrie asked as they fluttered onto his desk.

"Of course. I know every child's name—Little Big People and fairies."

Santa spoke softly. His voice didn't boom the way Arianna had described it. She'd said it made her fairy wings shake.

"Is something wrong?" Dorrie asked.

Trina noticed a rumpled letter in Santa's lap. "Did you get some bad news?"

Santa sighed. "Yes, I did. Here, read it for yourselves."

He propped the note against a lamp.

" 'Dear Santa, who doesn't live at the North Pole, or anywhere else for that matter,'" Trina read out loud. "'My mom and dad made me write this letter. But I don't believe in you. None of the kids in my school do. And none of my cousins or camp friends or anyone over the age of five does either. That's all! A real girl named Nina Connor.'"

"I've read this letter a hundred times," Santa explained. "And every time I read it, I feel worse. I'm sorry I haven't come out to meet your class, but I haven't wanted to leave this room all day. I just feel too bad."

"If you don't leave the room," Trina said, "how will you deliver the Christmas presents to all the Little Big People?"

Santa shrugged.

No wonder Clyde was nervous and the workshop elves were in such a frenzy!

"There won't even be a sleigh ride?" Dorrie yelped.

Santa shook his head.

"But then there won't be any Christmas," Trina said, her eyes opened wide.

"What difference does it make?" Santa sighed. "Nobody on Earth-Below believes in Christmas anyway."

"But, Santa," Dorrie said, trying to sound cheerful, "it's just one letter."

"True," Santa agreed. "It is just one letter. But Nina says her whole class doesn't believe, and everyone she knows!"

"You can't give up," Trina insisted. "You've been doing this forever!"

"And I'm tired," Santa told the fairies. "I need to know that my work means something. That people believe in me. Otherwise, it just isn't worth doing anymore."

He picked up the letter and began to read it again. Dorrie and Trina exchanged looks.

"But, Santa—" Dorrie began.

"Excuse me, little fairies." Mrs. Claus strode into the room. She was smiling, but Dorrie could tell she was worried. "It's time to join your class."

"Yes, ma'am," Trina said.

Dorrie flew up to Santa's cheek and kissed him lightly. "I hope you feel better," she said. Santa nodded, but Dorrie wasn't sure he'd even heard. He was too busy rereading the letter.

Outside the study, the fairies hovered in front of Mrs. Claus. "I'm sorry you had to see that," Mrs. Claus told them. "I've been trying to keep this all hush-hush. That's why I made up that excuse before, about Santa waxing the sleigh. Santa just hasn't been himself this holiday season."

"Maybe Ms. Periwinkle will know what to do," Trina said, remembering that the teacher had helped her many times.

Mrs. Claus shook her head. "Please don't

mention this to anyone. I don't want word to get around. Santa still has time to change his mind. And in the meantime, Clyde and all the elves are pitching in, trying get ready. Things may still work out. So I don't want anyone to feel scared or nervous. You must promise to keep this secret."

"We promise," the fairies said together.

Mrs. Claus ushered the fairies back to their classmates. Ms. Periwinkle was doing a wing count in front of the stables.

"Oh, there you are, Dorrie and Trina. We're just about to go home."

"Where have you been?" Belinda asked, hopping up and down in the snow.

"Oh, just wandering around," Trina answered quickly.

"Well, you missed the sleigh ride," said Laurel with a sneer. "Too bad for you. Now you'll never get a chance."

Dorrie would have loved the sleigh ride.

But right now she had something more im-
portant on her mind. "Let's meet back in
Fairyland, by the weeping willow tree," she
whispered to Trina. "Maybe we can think of
a way to help."

She looked at Ms. Periwinkle, then at Belinda and Olivia. She longed to tell them
about Santa. To ask them for ideas too. But
a promise was a promise, and she must keep
the secret.

Christmas might be canceled!

Chapter 4

Fluffy gray clouds hovered over Fairyland. Grown-up snow fairies were fluttering about, readying their snowflakes.

"It's going to be a white Christmas," Dorrie said to Trina as they sat under the weeping willow tree in Fairyland Meadow. "That is, if there *is* a—"

"Hush!" Trina interrupted. She waved a wing at Mr. Willow's branches.

"What's going on?" the tree sobbed. "I hate it when I don't know what's going on. Speak up and finish your sentence!"

"It's nothing," Mr. Willow," Dorrie said quickly. "We're just playing."

"We'd better go," Trina told Dorrie, and Dorrie nodded. They didn't want Mr. Willow to overhear anything else.

"See you later," they called as they slipped through his drooping branches and flew away.

"Boo-hoo," the tree wailed. "Have a merry Christmas."

The two fairies flitted above Fairyland Meadow, unsure where to go. They had to figure out a way to make Santa change his mind. They had to save Christmas!

"So, any ideas?" Dorrie asked hopefully as they hovered in the sky. If anyone would know what to do, it would be Trina.

Trina tugged on her pigtails, thinking. "We could go back to the North Pole. Talk to Santa again. Or help Mrs. Claus supervise the elves."

Then she sighed. "But we've already talked to Santa. And even if we help Mrs. Claus, only Santa can drive the sleigh."

Dorrie gulped. She blinked her eyes fast, not wanting to cry. No Christmas? It was just too terrible to think about.

"If only that Little Big Person had never sent that letter."

Trina clapped her wings. "That's it. Nina Connor! We can go to Earth-Below, find her, and convince her there really is a Santa Claus. *That* would make Santa feel better!"

Dorrie flapped her wings excitedly, almost going into a spin. Thank goodness for Trina. "Of course! Blitzen will know Nina's address. The reindeer know where all the Little Big

People live." Dorrie slowed her wings and added, "I wish we could tell Belinda and Olivia so they could come too."

"And our parents," Trina added sensibly. "But we promised to keep the secret."

A cuckoo-clock bird flew past. It was almost three o'clock. "We don't have much time before Santa has to start making his deliveries," Dorrie told Trina. "We should leave right away."

"Okay," Trina agreed. "But we still have to tell our parents something."

The two friends called for a messenger fairy to deliver two messages: one to the Windmists' tree-house, the other to the Larkspurs'. Dorrie and Trina would be playing in Fairyland Meadow all afternoon. But they would meet everyone at the Tree Decorating Party, a Christmas Eve celebration where all of Fairyland gathered by the tallest evergreen—the Big Tree.

"If we don't save Christmas by the time the party starts," Trina said, "we might as well forget the whole thing. It will be too late."

Cuckoo! Cuckoo! Cuckoo! Three o'clock.

"Let's fly!" Dorrie shouted.

Chapter 5

The fairies flew to Fairy School, where they quickly piled magic supplies into their fairy-packs. Then they flew as fast as they could to the North Pole.

"Hello!" Blitzen cried, surprised to see them.

Dorrie and Trina quickly explained their idea: to find Nina and persuade her to believe in Santa Claus. Then Santa would be happy, and it would be Christmas as usual. Trina knew just how to do this. She had a plan. But the fairies needed Blitzen's help first.

"Of course I know Nina's address!" Blitzen said. "In fact, I'll take you right to her house. That way, you'll get there quicker!"

"Good luck!" shouted Rudolph and the other reindeer as they flew away.

In no time at all, Blitzen landed gently on the roof of Nina's house. A plastic model of Santa and his reindeer stood right next to the chimney.

"Perfect!" Blitzen exclaimed. "I can wait for you right here, and no one will notice me."

"Thank you, Blitzen," Dorrie said, tumbling off his back.

"Now it's up to us!" Trina said, fluttering beside her.

The two fairies flew to a window and

peeked into the kitchen. "That must be Nina," Trina whispered to Dorrie.

Inside, they saw a Little Big Person about eight years old. She was with a smaller Little Big Person, who was placing cookies on a plate next to a big glass of milk.

"You're wasting your time," Nina was saying. "There is no Santa Claus."

Dorrie and Trina squeezed into the kitchen through a crack by the window. Quietly they flew behind a coffee can.

"Why bother leaving cookies for Santa?" Nina continued. "There is no Santa. And the sooner you know that, Max, the better. You're living in a dream world."

"Now what?" Dorrie whispered. "What's your plan, Trina?"

"We show ourselves to Nina," Trina said. "If she knows that fairies are real, she'll know Santa is real too."

"That's your great idea?" Dorrie asked slowly.

"Yes. Isn't it perfect?"

"But Trina, what about rule number one for visits to Earth-Below? Never, ever let a Big Person see you?"

"Well, I have a way to get around that." Trina rooted around in her fairypack and pulled out a jar labeled FORGET-ME DUST. "We'll just sprinkle this on Nina after she sees us, and she won't remember a thing. And if she truly believes—if we did a truly good job—then even after we sprinkle, the belief will stick like fairy glue."

"I don't know." Dorrie shook her head. It seemed so easy . . . too easy. If you could just sprinkle Forget-Me Dust on a Big Person, why would you even need rule one? But Trina was the smartest fairy she knew. If she thought it would work . . .

"Okay," Dorrie finally agreed. "But let's try it on Max first. If the fairy dust doesn't make him forget us, it won't be a big deal. He keeps telling Nina there's a Santa Claus, and she doesn't believe that. So I guess she wouldn't believe he'd seen fairies either."

They found Max in the family room, watching television. Dorrie flitted in front of the screen. "Hi, Max," she said. "My name is Dorrie."

Max gasped. "A fairy! A real live fairy!"

"That's right," said Trina, joining Dorrie. "Now you see us." She paused to toss the fairy dust, sprinkling it on Max's head. "And now you forget us."

She and Dorrie scooted behind a couch pillow.

Max shook the fairy dust out of his hair, then rubbed his eyes, looking confused.

"See?" Trina whispered. "He doesn't remember a thing."

"Dorrie?" Max called loudly. "Where are you?"

Dorrie's stomach flip-flopped. The fairy dust hadn't worked. She grabbed the jar from Trina and looked at it closely. "Read this!" she demanded, pointing out tiny print on the bottom of the label: WARNING: DOES NOT WORK FOR FAIRY MEMORIES.

Tina blushed. "Oops! I was in such a hurry, I didn't research this enough. I'm sorry, Dorrie."

"Dorrie! Dorrie!" Max was calling.

"I guess we just have to keep hiding," Dorrie said. "Maybe Max will lose interest if he doesn't see us again."

Max scampered out of the room and they followed, hiding behind furniture and pictures. "Nina!" he cried. "I saw a fairy!"

Nina was in her bedroom, stroking a fat orange cat. "Oh, Marmalade," she was sighing. "Why do people make such a big deal out of Christmas? It's such a sad holiday if your family isn't together." She looked up at her brother as he burst into the room.

"Fairies, Nina!" he cried.

"Santa Claus . . . fairies . . . what next, Max? A two-headed monster from Mars?"

Dorrie and Trina smiled. Dorrie was right. No one would believe Max. They were safe. But they still had to convince Nina that Santa was real.

"We need more fairy magic," Trina said softly, "to get her to believe."

"Okay," said Dorrie, rubbing her wings and thinking. What could they try next?

Chapter 6

What would make a Little Big Person believe in Christmas? Dorrie wondered. Suddenly she brightened. "It's against the rules for Santa's reindeer to talk to Nina," she told Trina. "But what if she sees Blitzen flying around? A flying reindeer! Then she'll believe!"

They hurried to the roof and explained their new idea to Blitzen.

"Sure," he said, readying his hooves for takeoff. "It's worth a try."

Dorrie and Trina flew back inside. They each tossed a handful of fairy dust over Nina. The dust spiraled around her, gently pulling her toward the window. Right outside, Blitzen was circling, waiting for Nina to spy him.

"Look!" Nina cried in delight to Max. "A flying reindeer!"

Dorrie grinned at Trina. They'd done it!

"Wow!" said Max. "It's one of Santa's reindeer."

"Don't be silly." Nina laughed. "It's just a reindeer kite!"

Disappointed, Dorrie and Trina signaled for Blitzen to hide once more. They had to come up with something else, Dorrie thought. Something that would make for a perfect Christmas day. What could it be?

"Snow!" she exclaimed. "That's what

everyone wants for the holiday—a white Christmas!"

"Good idea," said Trina. "But it has to seem like an extra-special snow. A magical flurry."

"I know!" Dorrie said. "It can snow indoors. Just over the family's Christmas tree in the living room."

"Great!" said Trina.

The fairies waited for Nina to go into the living room. Then Trina reached into her fairypack and drew out her magic wand. *"Let it snow for all to see. But keep the snow over the tree."*

Just as Nina passed the Christmas tree, a sprinkle of snowflakes fell over its branches. Nina stopped. The sprinkle turned into a flurry. Nina blinked.

"She thinks she's seeing things!" Dorrie whispered to Trina.

Nina stood still as a statue as the snow covered the branches—and only the branches. Then she shook her head as if to clear it.

"I'd better tell Mom and Dad," she said. "There's something wrong with the roof."

"Something wrong with the roof?" Dorrie moaned. "She doesn't think it's magic at all!"

The fairies tagged along as Nina headed to the study. Her mom was talking on the phone.

"But her mother will realize there's nothing wrong with the roof," Trina whispered, ducking behind the telephone stand and pulling Dorrie along with her. "And then Nina will know it's Christmas magic."

"Mom?" said Nina.

Her mother put one hand over the receiver. "Yes, dear? I'm talking to Grandma. Would you like to say hello?"

Quickly Nina reached for the telephone.

"She forgot about the snow!" Dorrie whispered while Nina spoke.

"Give her time," Trina advised.

"Okay," Nina was saying in a teary voice. "I guess I'll see you . . . when?" She listened for a moment. "Right. I'll see you soon." Again she listened. "Me too, Grandma."

She hung up the phone, then turned to her mother.

"Are you all right, dear?" her mother asked.

Nina nodded slowly. "I'm okay." She seemed about to say more, then changed her mind. "But, Mom, there's something wrong with the roof."

She led her mother to the Christmas tree. Mrs. Connor eyed the snow-covered tree and the flakes still floating down. Marmalade the cat had padded over and was now sleeping peacefully at the tree's foot.

"How odd," Mrs. Connor said. "I'd better call the roof repair person." She dialed the phone but hung up a moment later. The company was already closed for the holiday.

"You know," she said, looking at the pretty

43

scene, "it's not so bad. In fact, it's kind of Christmassy. And the ceiling seems to be holding up fine. The repairs can wait."

Dorrie's wings wilted. The Big People all thought it was just a roof problem. And they wouldn't be able to check it until Christmas was over.

"Well, that didn't work," she told Trina, waving her wand to turn off the snow.

Trina shrugged. "Let's try something different. What else do people like about Christmas?"

"Music!" Dorrie exclaimed. Quickly she re-cited another spell: "*Music here, music there, Christmas music in the air.*" Instantly holiday carols piped through the house.

Nina sighed and reached for a book. "Those cars outside are playing music so loud!" she said. "I hope I can concentrate enough to read!"

Nina thought the music was from passing cars! Nothing seemed to be working.

"I don't know," Dorrie said, fluttering her wings sadly. "Maybe we should just forget—"

"Watch out!" Trina whispered. "You're going to bump into the cat!"

"Ouch!" Marmalade yowled. "I thought fairies were supposed to be graceful."

"Most are," Dorrie laughed. "But I guess I'm special that way."

"Well," the cat grumbled, "be more careful next time. I need my afternoon catnap."

"But it's almost Christmas," Dorrie said. "You should be too excited to sleep."

The cat yawned. "Christmas, Shmistmas. Why shouldn't I sleep? I already met Santa, last Christmas Eve, right here in front of the tree."

"Marmalade," they heard Nina call. "Where are you?"

45

"I know!" Dorrie said suddenly. "Let's cast a spell so Nina understands the cat. Then *he* can tell her about Santa."

The cat snored. He was already fast asleep and didn't notice Trina sprinkling fairy dust on him.

A second later, Nina scooped him up. "There you are!"

"Yes, I'm here," the cat snapped. "And I'd like to stay here, fast asleep, please!"

"What?" Surprised, Nina dropped him on the floor.

"Nina can understand you, Marmalade," Dorrie whispered, peeking out from behind the couch. "Tell her about Santa."

"Why should I?" the cat hissed back in a low voice. "Santa stepped on my tail last Christmas and woke me up. Believe me, it's no fun having a big guy like that walk all over you. My tail still hurts!"

"Marmalade?" Nina said, bending over the cat. Dorrie scooted back into hiding. "Did you really say something?"

"Purrrr," said the cat.

"Oh, he's refusing to talk!" Trina sighed. "This isn't working either."

"Come on, Marmalade," Nina begged. "I thought I heard you say something!"

"Meow."

Dorrie glanced at the setting sun. Marmalade wasn't about to help. And time was running out!

Chapter 7

The fairies flew to a wreath hanging above the fire and settled down in its leaves to talk.

"We need to figure something out fast," Trina said.

Dorrie tugged at her curls. "More than anything in Fairyland, I want there to be a Christmas. That's my Christmas wish." Suddenly she lifted her head. "I have it! I have another idea."

"What is it?" Trina asked eagerly.

"We find out what Nina really wants. I mean, really, truly wants in her heart of hearts for Christmas. It has to be something she hasn't told anyone. Something so special that when we give it to her, she'll realize there really is someone magical granting Christmas wishes!"

"Okay!" Trina jumped up. "We have about an hour left. So we'll follow Nina everywhere she goes, and maybe she'll give us some sort of clue."

The fairies flitted quickly to Nina's room. They watched her read a book. They watched her watch TV.

Dorrie yawned. This wasn't getting them anywhere. And it was boring!

Finally they followed her into the kitchen and watched her eat a cheese sandwich.

"Mom will be mad," Max said, skipping

into the room. "That's going to spoil your appetite, and you won't want any dinner."

"I'm hungry now," Nina answered back. "And it's none of your business."

Max stuck out his tongue. "I'm going to tell," he said in a singsong voice, hurrying out of the room. "And you can't stop me!"

"Hey, Max!" Nina called out quickly in a sweet voice. "Want to play?"

Max stopped in his tracks. "With you?"

"Of course with me. There's no one else here."

"What about those two little fairies?" Max said.

"There *aren't* any fairies!" Nina snapped.

Max's lip quivered. "You're mean. I'm going to tell Mom, and you're going to be in big—"

Nina leaped up and put her arm around her brother. "I'm sorry, Max. Listen, what would you like to do? I'll play anything you say."

Max brightened. "Let's play Old Maid!"

"Old Maid?" Nina repeated. "That's what we always play with Grandma and Grandpa."

"I know. But they're not coming this year."

Nina found the card game and took Max into the living room. She spread the cards on the carpet. "It doesn't seem right to play without Grandma and Grandpa here."

"I know," Max said.

"More than anything in the world," Nina went on, "I wish they could come for Christmas. But they've moved so far away, they can't make the trip."

Dorrie poked Trina with her wing. "That's it! Nina's greatest wish. To see her grandparents!"

Chapter 8

Dorrie and Trina raced to the roof.

"Blitzen!" Dorrie said excitedly. "We need your help again! Where do Nina's grandparents live?"

"And can you take us there?" Trina added.

"Of course!" Blitzen leaped into the air. "In two shakes of a reindeer's tail."

Blitzen streaked across the sky. Soon he

swooped down beside a little white house and crouched behind a hedge. Daylight was fading, turning to dusk. For the first time, Dorrie was glad it was getting late. The growing darkness would make it difficult for people to spot the reindeer in his hiding place.

"We don't have much time," Dorrie whispered. "How do we get the grandparents back to Nina's house?"

"We'll all ride on Blitzen," Trina answered. "Follow me!" She led Blitzen up the back steps, then rapped on the door with her magic wand. The door swung open and the fairies scooted behind Blitzen.

"Is someone there?" called a voice. Nina's grandparents stepped into the doorway.

"Oh, my!" the grandmother said. "It's a reindeer."

Before Nina's grandparents could turn back inside to call the local zoo or the police,

Trina tossed some fairy dust. It whirled around the grandparents, sweeping them gently off the ground and depositing them on Blitzen's back.

"Hold on tight!" the reindeer whispered to Dorrie and Trina, who were clinging to his fur. "Next stop, the Connor house!"

The moon peeked out from behind dark clouds as Blitzen coasted to a stop in Nina's backyard. Dorrie could see Nina and her family through a window, setting the dining room table for a special holiday dinner.

Nina glanced up. A reindeer was standing in her backyard—with her grandparents on his back! She dropped a glass. Then she raced to open the back door.

"Wh-wh-what's going on?" she stammered. Max and her parents hurried to her side.

"This very kind flying reindeer brought us

here to celebrate Christmas with you," her grandmother said calmly.

"But that's my Christmas wish! And it came true!"

Nina rushed into her grandparents' arms and hugged them tight. "I can't believe you're really here. This is the most wonderful thing I can think of." She turned to smile at Max. "Maybe you're right about Santa."

She petted Blitzen. "And you're real too—a real flying reindeer, not a kite! This is so amazing!"

"Well, well, well," said Mrs. Connor. "Today seems to be full of Christmas miracles. Everyone, come inside. It's getting cold."

"Good-bye," they all called to the reindeer. "Thank you!"

"You know what I'm going to do?" Nina said to Max as everyone settled in front of a roaring fire in the living room. "I'm going to

write Santa another letter and tell him I changed my mind. I do believe in him."

She jumped up to get a paper and pen.

Dorrie fluttered her wings excitedly. This was it! They'd bring the letter to Santa and cheer him up! She giggled and wiggled and flapped—and bumped into Trina.

"Oops!" said Trina. The Forget-Me Dust toppled out of her fairypack, sprinkling Nina's head as she picked up a pen.

"Oh, no!" Dorrie gasped. Nina wouldn't remember Blitzen; she wouldn't remember anything. Would she still believe in Santa Claus? Would she still write the letter?

Dorrie crossed her wings for luck and waited.

Chapter 9

Nina held the piece of paper in her hand. She gazed at it, puzzled. "What am I doing with this?" she asked.

Dorrie sighed. "She's forgotten everything. We might as well sprinkle the Forget-Me Dust over everyone else now too, so Nina doesn't think they've all gone crazy."

Trina nodded. "Here goes," she said, scattering the dust over the rest of the family.

"Was I going to write something?" Nina went on, putting down the paper. Then she glanced at her grandparents, who were talking quietly with her parents.

"The plane trip was so quick, I can't even remember a thing," her grandfather was saying. "No crowds, no waiting. It was amazing!"

Max stepped close to Nina. "You were going to write a letter to Santa."

"Of course, *he* remembers the letter," Dorrie whispered, "because he's believed in Santa all along."

"I was going to write to Santa?" Nina laughed.

"Oh, Nina, dear," her grandmother said. "We have time to play one round of Old Maid before dinner."

Nina smiled. Their special card game!

"I'll be right there," she told her grandmother. "I just have one thing to do."

She sat at a desk in the corner. "Dear Santa," she wrote. "A Christmas miracle happened today. My grandparents came to visit! Seeing them has made me believe in holiday magic—and in you. I do believe in you, Santa, and if you had anything to do with bringing my grandparents here, I'd like to thank you. Your friend, Nina."

She left the note by the fireplace, next to Max's plate of cookies.

"How about that game now?" she said to her grandparents.

The entire family began to play. Dorrie nodded to Trina, and then the fairies lifted the letter together. They would show it to Santa. Let him read that one girl believed in him.

"Another ride on Blitzen!" Dorrie declared. "This time, to the North Pole!"

Knock, knock! Dorrie pounded on the door of Santa's house. "Special delivery!" she called. "One letter for Santa."

Mrs. Claus opened the door. "Why, Dorrie, Trina," she said. "What are you doing here?"

"We brought this letter," Trina said. "And we think Santa should see it—now!"

The fairies hurried to Santa's study. He was dozing, Nina's first letter still in his hand.

Dorrie fluttered her wings by his nose. *"Aaachooo!"* Santa sneezed, waking up.

They held the letter in front of his nose like a banner. A few seconds later, a slow smile spread over his face.

"My goodness! Nina believes in Christmas after all. I don't know what happened to change her mind, but this makes me so happy I could …"

"Go for a sleigh ride?" Trina suggested.

"Deliver Christmas presents?" Dorrie added.

Santa jumped to his feet. "I'd better get

moving, before it's Christmas day and too late for anything!"

Dorrie and Trina flew beside Santa as he rushed to the workshop. The elves were slumped over their worktable, exhausted. Clyde snored gently, fast asleep, a red bow in one hand, a red ribbon in the other. Presents were half wrapped. Nuts and bolts lay scattered over the floor, and outside, Santa's sleigh stood empty.

Santa clapped his hands. "On your feet!" he cried. "It's Christmas Eve! We've got our work cut out for us!"

"We'll help," Dorrie offered.

"Ho, ho, ho," Santa laughed merrily, sounding like his old self. "Some fairy magic is just what we need."

Dorrie and Trina held hands. They had to use powerful magic now, to finish up the work.

"*Christmas Eve is almost here. We have to spread some Christmas cheer. Let's get ready, set things right, it's almost time for Santa's flight.*"

They waved their magic wands once, twice, three times. Suddenly the presents jumped to attention. Wrapping paper folded itself around boxes and gifts. Tools flew neatly into drawers and shelves. And Santa's giant toy bag sailed into the room, landing on top of the table. One by one, the presents hopped inside.

"Well," said Clyde. "That's done." He reached for a list and checked off the last items. "Now there's only one thing left to do."

"It's already done," Mrs. Claus called from outside. "Come look, Santa, dear. Your sleigh is waiting."

Everyone trooped outside, and there stood

Santa's sleigh, glistening in the moonlight, all the reindeer in their harnesses.

Blitzen winked at Dorrie and Trina. "Ready when you are, Santa."

Santa kissed Mrs. Claus, shook hands with all the elves, then turned to Dorrie and Trina. "Your fairy magic got the job done so quickly, we have time for a little detour. Would you like a ride back to Fairyland?"

"Would we ever!" said Dorrie.

Dorrie and Trina perched on Santa's shoulder for the moonlit ride. Soon the familiar trees, lakes, and fields of Fairyland spread out below them. A fine snow was falling, covering the land like a cozy blanket.

"Can you take us to the Big Tree?" asked Dorrie. "We have a decorating party to go to."

"Sure," said Santa, just as he flew over Laurel's tree-house.

The mean little fairy was fluttering on a branch. "Come on," she was shouting to her parents. "I want to get to the party before all the fairy punch is gone!"

"Hi, Laurel!" Dorrie cried. "We got to take a sleigh ride after all!"

"What? How did you manage—" Laurel sputtered, the rest of her words lost as the sleigh sped away. Dorrie grinned.

A second later, they arrived at the Big Tree. The reindeer slowed to a stop, hovering over the fairies, bugs, and birds, who were all decorating the giant evergreen.

It was time to say good-bye.

"Merry Christmas, Santa," said Dorrie as she and Trina flew from Santa's shoulder. "Merry Christmas, reindeer!"

"And thank you for the ride," Trina added.

"Ho, ho, ho," Santa said. "I should be thanking you. If you hadn't helped, there wouldn't have been a Christmas at all."

He smiled at the fairies, and the sleigh took off, disappearing among the stars.

"Well, let's see what's going on!" Dorrie said to Trina.

They flew a few branches down.

"Dorrie! Trina!" Belinda shouted. She somersaulted into the air beside them. "Come on! Olivia and I are decorating this branch right here."

"And we have lots of pretty ornaments left for you!" Olivia added, fluttering quietly to their side. She waved to a stack of Christmas ornaments floating in the breeze.

Dorrie and Trina picked a big bright red one and hung it up together. They looked at each other and grinned.

"There'll never be another Christmas quite like this one," Trina said.

Dorrie nodded. "Happy holidays, everyone. And a special Merry Christmas to you, Nina Connor," she whispered. "May all your Christmas wishes come true!"

The Fairy School Pledge

(sung to the tune of "Twinkle, Twinkle, Little Star")

We are fairies
Brave and bright.
Shine by day,
Twinkle by night.

We're friends of birds
And kind to bees.
We love flowers
And the trees.

We are fairies
Brave and bright.
Shine by day,
Twinkle by night.